Eli and Mort's Epic Adventures
Breckenridge

About this project

The idea for Eli and Mort's Epic Adventures Series came from the joy we experienced watching our kids ski, snowboard and have the time of their lives growing up in the mountains. We wanted to share that joy and the beauty of the mountains with the world. We decided to write a series of books through the eyes of a child on an epic adventure -- a series of books for adventuring kids like you! This is the fourth book in the Series, "Eli and Mort's Epic Adventures Breckenridge."

When considering the concept we imagined what a child might see and feel when they stood at the top of the mountain about to take the first run of the day, and thought, 'Who better qualified to illustrate the book than the children that live here'? As a result, we agreed that the background illustrations should be drawn by the children of Summit County.

About the characters

Eli, a 5-year-old boy, and his pal Mort the Moose are the best of friends exploring the world together. When others are around Mort is a stuffed moose but to Eli, Mort is his best friend and partner in fun. In this book, they are experiencing all that Breckenridge has to offer.

Eli and Mort are dedicated to the loves of our lives,
Josh, Heath & Will.

Enjoy!

Created by Elyssa Pallai and Ken Nager
Published by Resort Books Ltd.
Background illustrations by the children of Summit County
Character Illustrations by Eduardo Paj
Background Cover image by Emilie McAtamney
All rights reserved by Resort Books Ltd. 2015, including the right of reproduction in whole or in part in any form.
Text and illustrations copyright © 2015 by Resort Books Ltd.

Printed in Korea
October 2015

Thank you

We love our friends in Breckenridge. Mort and I think you are AWESOME! Special thanks to Eduardo Paj for making us look so good, Nicole Magistro from the Bookworm who inspired us to write this, Brent and Barb Bingham at PhotoFX and Brenda Himelfarb and Diane Pallai for making sure what we wrote was what we meant to write. "Hooray!" to all of the AWESOME children who illustrated this book and their parents. Special thanks to Breckenridge Creative Arts for their ongoing support in helping us reach the world.

Visit **eliandmort.com** to order our latest adventure, check out our events or to just say, "Hi!"

A portion of the proceeds of this book go to Breckenridge Creative Arts.

The Illustrators

Eli and Mort would like to thank the AMAZING local children, ages 7 to 17, that illustrated the backgrounds! Below are some of their favorite things to do in Breckenridge. What's yours?

D

Ethan Fulkerson
The Peak School
15 years old
Favorite: Skiing with friends & walking around town

I

Sophia Elsass
Seton Home Study School
12 years old
Favorite: Any sports, clay sculpting, animation, ski racing, hiking, geo-caching & birding

E

Kathryn Goettelman
South Park High School
14 years old
Favorite: Skiing

J

Ella Eland
Summit Middle School
11 years old
Favorite: Visiting the South Ranch Library with my family & friends

A

Selah Kreeger
The Peak School
16 years old
Favorite: Theater, piano, skiing, fencing, cello, hiking & climbing

F

Tahley Scott
Lafayette High School
14 years old
Favorite: Snowboarding

K

Lexi Stais
Breckenridge Elementary
7 years old
Favorite: Skiing, sleding & having fun

B

Emilie McAtamney
Summit Middle School
13 years old
Favorite: Skiing, events & going into town

G

Sam TheBeau
Summit Middle School
11 years old
Favorite: Hiking, skiing, biking into town & soccer

L

Chase Byers
Summit High School
13 years old
Favorite: Walking down Main Street on a warm, sunny day with friends

C
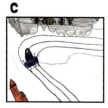
Cole Robertson
Breckenridge Elementary
8 years old
Favorite: Skiing, mountain biking, going to school, playing with friends & whitewater rafting

H

Keelie Rix
Summit High School
16 years old
Favorite: Volunteering with the BOEC

M

Jordan Ruigrok
Hulstrom K-8
10 years old
Favorite: Hiking, biking & skiing

N 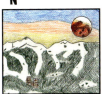 **Halston Van Loan**
Summit Middle School
11 years old
Favorite: Walking around town & sharing memories

T  **Auden Pierpont**
Breckenridge Elementary
7 years old
Favorite: Biking

Z  **Shelby Stais**
Breckenridge Elementary
9 years old
Favorite: Skiing, sledding & art

O  **Mari McAtamney**
Summit High School
15 years old
Favorite: Meeting friends downtown, hiking & rafting

U  **Karlyn Frazier**
Upper Blue Elementary
9 years old
Favorite: Swimming

Outtakes 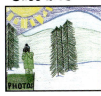 **Grace Frank**
Summit High School
17 years old
Favorite: Sunny, fresh powder days

P  **Lily Hess**
Summit Middle School
11 years old
Favorite: Skiing, art & going to Fuzzywig's

V  **Jarelle Bjork**
The Peak School
15 years old
Favorite: Walking around & looking at the lights and people

Outtakes  **Rhiannon Myers**
Summit High School
17 years old
Favorite: Skiing

Q **Joey Goldstein**
University School
10 years old
Favorite: Skiing

W **Harbor T. Scheuermann**
Breckenridge Elementary
8 years old
Favorite: Dirt biking, skiing, snowboarding, hip-hop, football & having fun

R **Gracie Eland**
Summit High School
13 years old
Favorite: Playing hockey

X **Katie Mason**
Summit High School
16 years old
Favorite: Walking around Main Street during Christmas with all the pretty lights

S  **Charlotte Hudnut**
Dillon Valley Elementary
9 years old
Favorite: Drawing & swimming

Y **Ella Piecoup**
Summit High School
16 years old
Favorite: Hiking, backcountry skiing Whale's Tail & nordic skiing

A is for arriving at **Denver International Airport**. When my stepmom, dad, li'l sis, Mort the Moose and I arrived we saw mountains everywhere. Even the airport roof looked like snowcapped mountains and teepees way up high in the Colorado blue sky. And as the plane floated down and touched the ground our adventure in Breckenridge began!

B is for **Breckenridge.** My dad told us Breckenridge was an old mining town and there was gold under the streets. So Mort and I put on our mining gear and began digging for gold under the snow. We found rocks that sparkled in the sun. "It's gold!" I said to Mort. He agreed. My stepmom smiled and put the rocks in her pocket for later.

Cole Robertson

C is for the **Gold Runner Alpine Coaster** on Breckenridge Mountain. Mort and I had been on a regular roller coaster in the summer, but never on an alpine coaster in the snow. "Whoopie!" we screamed, laughed and lost our breath as we zoomed all the way down the mountain - even faster than the fastest skier or snowboarder.

D is for **Daylight Doughnuts** where you can eat breakfast for lunch in Breckenridge. Most of the time my stepmom made us eat healthy food, but when we were on an adventure, she let us eat donuts. I liked chocolate frosted donuts with sprinkles the best. Mort and I picked the sprinkles off one by one to make the donuts last longer. Yummm!

E is for **Eric's Downstairs**. Eric's is a restaurant with everything kids like to eat and lots of video games. Mort and I would rather play video games than eat, but we never had enough quarters. I would ask my stepmom, "One more quarter PLEEEEEASE." My asking usually worked on my stepmom...but not as much on my dad.

F is for **Fuzzywig's Candy Factory** where we bought gobstoppers that were bigger than our heads. I said to Mort, "This is better than gold, it's candy!" Mort thought so too. Yep-a-doodle-doo!

G is for the **Breck Connect Gondola** that connects the town of Breckenridge to the ski mountain. It was our second favorite ride on the mountain after the Gold Runner Coaster. We listened as the gondola click clacked its way up the mountain and held on tightly as it swayed back and forth, back and forth.

H is for the **Haunted Forest** ski run. Mort and I had our ski poles ready to defend my li'l sis as we skied through the mine shaft entrance of the Haunted Forest. Sure enough my li'l sis screamed at the FIRST SCARY THING! It was a giant, blow-up spider! "Whoo-hoo!" my li'l sis laughed as she skied under the spider and through to the other side.

I is for **Imperial Express SuperChair**. My dad told us it was the highest chairlift in North America. My stepmom DEFINITELY wasn't going to the top, top, top of the mountain. Neither was I, or my li'l sis. I gave my dad Mort for good luck. Just to be sure they were safe, I waited at the bottom of the chairlift until they came down.

J is for **Jump**. Mort and I were tired from saving my li'l sis and waiting for my dad. We decided to sit on the deck and pretend we were judges rating the skiers and snowboarders as they caught huge air. "10!" Mort and I cheered. Yahoo!

K is for **Kids Adventure Zones**. Kids Adventures Zones were ski runs made especially for kids. At the entrance there was a sign that said, "No parents allowed without a child." My dad said that was ironic. I wasn't sure what ironic meant. Mort wasn't sure either. But we both thought it was a funny rule.

L is for **Look**. My Dad told us that safety on the mountain was important so everyone could have fun and not get hurt. One rule he told us was to always LOOK up the mountain to see if someone was coming down before we started to ski again. Being safe made me feel good. Mort felt good too.

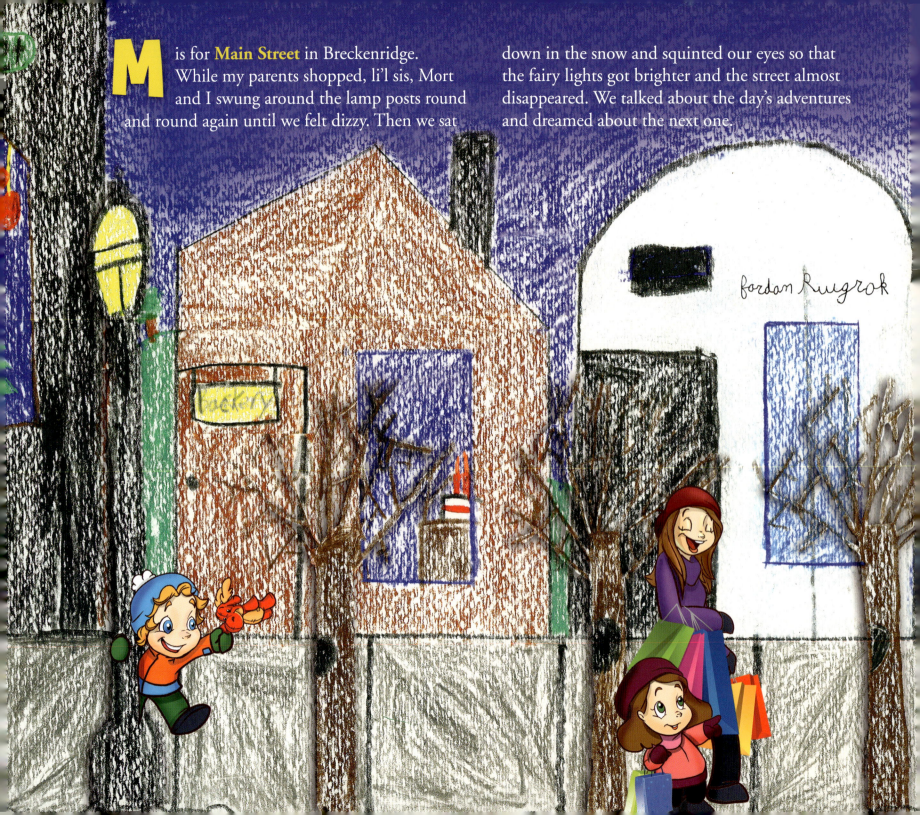

M is for **Main Street** in Breckenridge. While my parents shopped, li'l sis, Mort and I swung around the lamp posts round and round again until we felt dizzy. Then we sat down in the snow and squinted our eyes so that the fairy lights got brighter and the street almost disappeared. We talked about the day's adventures and dreamed about the next one.

N is for **Night Sky**. Mort and I looked up and saw the moon was bigger than our heads and was glowing the color of red raspberry ice cream. My dad told me it was called a blood moon. "What's a blood moon?" I asked. My dad said a blood moon happens when the Earth casts its shadow on a full moon. I shadowed Mort to see if he would turn redder in my shadow, but it was hard to tell since he was already mostly red.

O is for being **Outside**. A man from the hotel told Mort and me that it was a "bluebird day." We imagined there must be bluebirds everywhere so we sat on the chairs outside Ten Mile Station and waited for them to arrive. The sky was bluer than blue and the snow was piled high like pillows for us to jump around in and explore.

P is for the **Snow Plow** at Rotary Snowplow Park. Mort and I thought about giant waterfalls of snow blowing off the tracks while we played. "Woo-woo!" I tooted while Mort chugga chug chugged. Together we sounded like a real train.

Q is for **Mount Quandary,** a fourteener you can see from Breckenridge. My stepmom told us Mount Quandary is called a Fourteener because its peak is higher than 14,000 feet. In Colorado there are 58 mountains that are taller than 14,000 feet. Mount Quandary is one of the tallest of them all.

R is for **Restaurant**. Our favorite was Fatty's Pizzeria as Mort's favorite food, of course, is pizza. Mine too. Yahoo! After doing so many awesome runs on the mountain, we all jumped for joy at the thought of pizza for dinner at Fatty's.

S is for **Snow Sculptures** that are made from ice and snow at the snow sculpture competition. Artists use picks and saws and all sorts of tools to make art out of snow. Mort and I pretended we were sitting inside our favorite one…the monster truck in the snow. Whoa!

T is for **Terrain Park**. Terrain parks are built with jumps and boxes for skiers and snowboarders to practice their tricks. In Breckenridge there are easy, medium and hard ones. We started at an easy one, and then when we were ready, we tried our skills at a medium one to catch some more air and practice our box slides. Whoo-hoo!

U is for **Ullr Fest**. At Ullr Fest there were all sorts of wild and silly people dressed in lots of crazy costumes. Ullr is the god of snow. Mort and I squished all the way to the front of the crowd to grab as much candy as possible. Apparently the god of snow likes candy too. Mort yelled, "Booyah!" as he stuffed as much candy as he could in his snow hat.

V is for the beautiful **View** from the top of Breckenridge. On top of the mountain Mort and I shared the view with a boy we didn't know. "Do you want to ride with us?" I asked our new friend. The boy said, "Sure." And with that, Mort, our new friend and I snowboarded down the mountain together.

W is for the **Wind** on Lake Dillon, where snowkiters fly with kites in the wind, and catch big air off of frozen jumps. I thought it looked really fun. So did Mort. We decided maybe we'd try it next year.

X is for the **eXpert Ski Instructors** at the Ski and Ride School in Breckenridge. I listened to my li'l sis sing out loud as she worked on carving her turns back and forth, back and forth. She said singing helped her concentrate.

Y is for **Yard Sale**. My stepmom told us that when someone falls down and loses their skis on the slope it's called a "yard sale." Mort and I passed time on the lift trying to find skiers on the slope that had just had a yard sale. I told Mort we should help them find their skis on the way down. Mort thought so too.

Z is for **Zooming** down the Four O'clock ski run at the end of the day, the longest ski run on Breckenridge Mountain. Mort and I were very hungry after so much skiing that we rode down the mountain as fast as we could. My stepmom and dad yelled after us, "Slow down!" So we did. We couldn't wait until our next adventure!

Outtakes

There was so much more to do in Breckenridge.

See you in Park City
on our next adventure!

Check out our other adventures at
www.eliandmort.com

Beaver Creek

Vail   Vail-en Espanol

Steamboat   Learn to Snowboard 1, 2, 3